LAURENT DE BRUNHOFF

BABAR'S
World Tour

HARRY N. ABRAMS, INC., PUBLISHERS

"Pack a sweater, a bathing suit, and a pair of pyjamas. Wear comfortable shoes," Babar said to his children one morning. "Your mother and I have a surprise for you. We are taking you around the world!"

"You will see places different from Celesteville and ways of life that are different from the one you know," said Celeste.

That very afternoon, suitcases were loaded into the car that took them to the airport.

The children followed their parents aboard Elephant One. Cornelius was left in charge of Celesteville.

Babar and Celeste had equipped the plane with a library and language CDs, so the children could learn to say hello in each of the countries they were visiting.

When the family was settled, with their seat belts fastened, the plane took off. The first stop would be Italy.

"In Italy," Babar explained, "you do not say 'hello.' You say, 'Buon giorno!' BWONE JOOR-NO! Repeat after me."

"Bwone joor-no!" said the children.

"Very good. Again. Louder!"

"BWONE JOOR-NO!"

"Buon giorno," said the children at a street café in Rome.

"Buon giorno!" replied the waiter. "What would you like? Some pasta?"

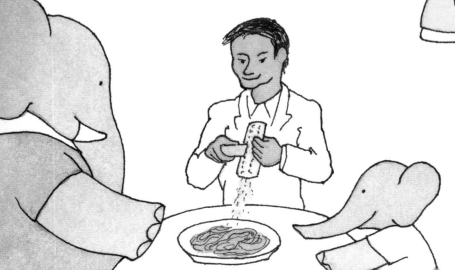

"In Italy, the food is good," said Celeste. "Si mangia bene!
SEE MON-JA BENNY!"

"See mon-ja benny!" said the children.

"Si!" said the waiter. "In Italia, si mangia bene!"

The family went to see the Coliseum and the Forum, and then it was time to leave Rome.

"Say, 'Arrivederci, Roma.' Ah-ree-va-dare-chee, Row-mah. . . .

"Cool!" said Pom. "Pasta! Venezia! Arrivederci!"

In Germany, they learned to say, "Guten Tag!"
In Spain they took a flamenco lesson and said, "Buenos dias!"
"Why don't they just say 'hello'?" Isabelle wanted to know.
"What's wrong with our words?"

"Nothing's wrong with our words," Celeste explained, laughing. "That's just how it is. People in different places say things differently. They do things differently, too. They build different kinds of buildings. They sleep in different kinds of beds. That's the fun of travelling. Did you ever see a building like this one in Celesteville?"
And the children had to admit they had not.

МЕТРО

Парк

МОСКВа

кремль

That same day they were in Russia, where the signs said "Парк" when they meant "Park," and the children learned to say "DOSS VEE-DONE-YA" instead of "Good-bye!"

"You see," said Babar, "here they don't even use the same alphabet we do."

"Doss vee-done-ya!" said the children. "That's 'good-bye.' 'Spah-see-bo' is 'thank you.'"

They thought foreign languages were fun, like singing different songs for different places. In chorus, the children shouted, "Pasta, Venezia, arrivederci! Guten Tag! Buenos dias!"

The children soon met with manners and customs unfamiliar to them, just as Celeste had told them they would.

In India, even the elephants dressed differently. Babar and his family met with some local representatives.

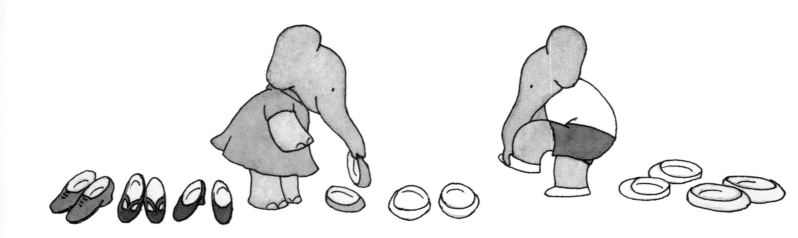

In Japan, Babar, Celeste, and the children took off their shoes when they went indoors.

They sat on the floor and used chopsticks when they ate. At the end of a meal, they bowed to their host and said, "GO CHEE SO SA MA! What a good meal!"

They went to a garden of sand and stone, and sat very quietly. This was called meditating.

There was so much to remember when you travelled! Just being polite was hard work. To relax from their efforts, Babar, Celeste, and the children went to southern Thailand for some wonderful snorkelling.

In Thailand, to show respect, people put their palms together, fingers up, and said, "SA WA DEE." If you made a mistake, the Thais did not get upset. They were always saying, "MY PEN RYE," which meant "No problem."

When everyone was rested, they went to Angkor in Cambodia, the ancient city of the Khmers.

In Mexico, they climbed a pyramid built by the Aztecs.

In both places, the original settlers were gone but tourists abounded.

"Will everyone move out of Celesteville one day, too?" Pom asked.

"Never," said Babar. "But apart from us, it happens a lot, as you'll see."

They then visited the cliff houses of the Anasazi in the high desert of the American Southwest.

They walked the Inca Trail, on the same stones that the Incas had walked . . .

. . . to the remains of the city of Machu Picchu hidden in the Andes Mountains.

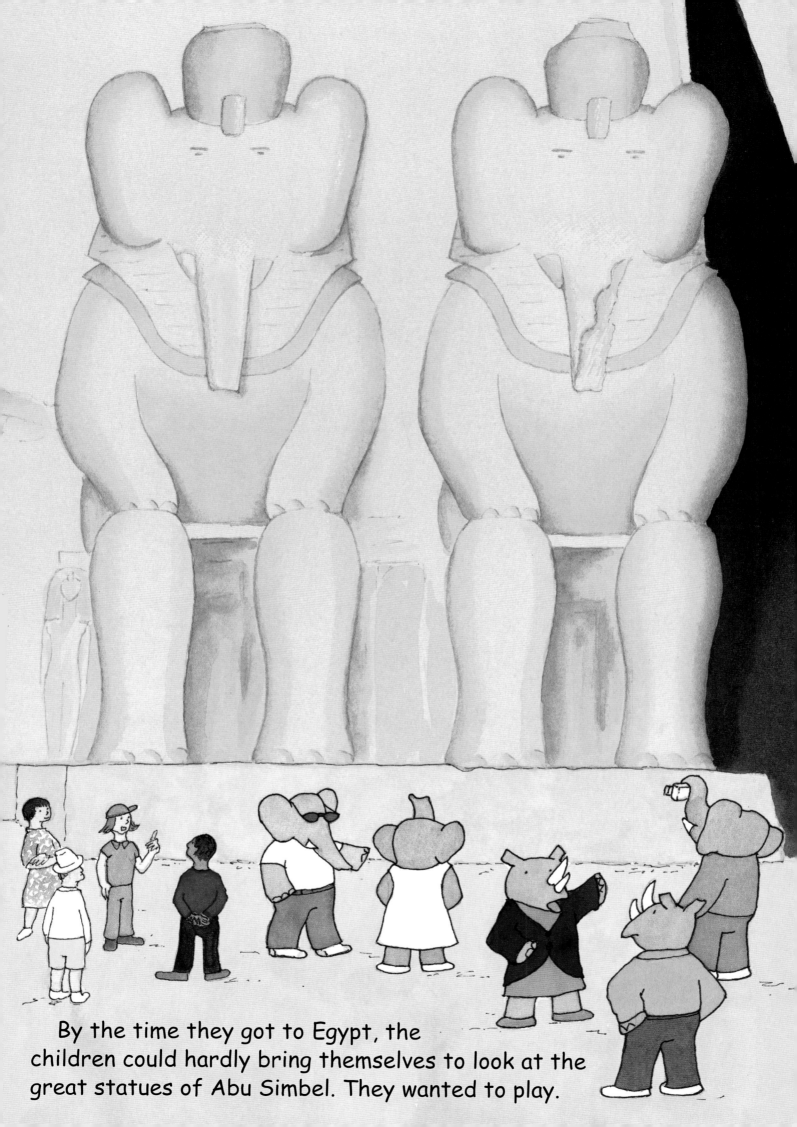

By the time they got to Egypt, the children could hardly bring themselves to look at the great statues of Abu Simbel. They wanted to play.

"I think the children are getting tired," said Celeste.
"Nonsense," said Babar. "They haven't been to France yet. BONE-JOOR, PAH-REE!"
"Bone-joor, Pah-ree," repeated the children dutifully.

Babar took them to see the Cathedral of Notre Dame.

Then he took them to a fashion show.
"The French dress beautifully, OWN SA-BEE BYEN
ON FRANCE," said Babar.

The children did not want to say, "On s'habille bien en France." They laughed at the dresses in the fashion show.

Babar and Celeste took them to a grassy square with buildings around it. They said they always came to this spot when they were in Paris.

"After the palace at Celesteville," said Babar, "this square may be the most agreeable place in any city in the world."

"There aren't even swings," said Isabelle. "Our house is nicer. When are we going home?"

"But we must see Antarctica," said Babar. So they flew to Patagonia and got on a ship and made their way to the land of the penguins. A small rubber boat took them from the big ship to the icebergs.

Pom and Alexander wanted to stay on the ship to play Ping-Pong, skipping the icebergs, but Babar said no.

"You can play Ping-Pong at home, but you can't see icebergs," Babar pointed out.

"At home we don't have a Ping-Pong table," replied Alexander.

So Babar finally realized that the children had had enough travel, and he told the pilot to take them home to Celesteville.

A week later, the family showed slides of their world tour
to their closest friends, including Cornelius and the Old Lady.

"What a wonderful trip!" everyone said.

"Yes," said Isabelle contentedly. "You can't imagine what beautiful clothes they have in France."

"When I grow up, I'm going to be a flamenco dancer," said Flora.

"In Spain, they don't eat dinner until midnight," Pom explained to the Old Lady.

"Many things are handled differently outside of Celesteville," said Alexander.

The children couldn't wait to take another family trip. In the meantime, they played Ping-Pong on the new table which, by coincidence, Cornelius had installed in the palace while they were travelling.

Production Manager: Jonathan Lopes

ISBN 0-8109-5982-8

Printed and bound in China
10 9 8 7 6 5 4 3 2 1

Harry N. Abrams, Inc.
100 Fifth Avenue
New York, NY 10011
www.abramsbooks.com

Abrams is a subsidiary of